Munch, Munch, Munch!

Written by Julie Penn

Illustrated by Camilla Galindo

Collins

Who and what is in this story?

Listen and say

Bill

Jim

plane

train

What is for lunch?
Munch, munch, munch!

Bread and chicken,
Fish and rice.

What is for lunch?
Munch, munch, munch!

Eggs and potatoes,
This is nice!

Do you like apples?
Yes, I do!

Do you like cake?
I like that, too!

What is for lunch?
Munch, munch, munch!

I have got a robot.
I have got a plane.

I have got a flower.
I have got a train.

This is funny!
I like this game.

I have got a football,
I have got a cat.

Here is a little man ...
With a hat!

I see carrots.
I see bread.

Look, an apple
For a head!

I like buses.

I like trees.

You like bread,
And you like cheese!

We like fruit,
And we like meat!

We like carrots,
Time to eat!
Munch, munch, munch!

Picture dictionary

Listen and repeat

apple

bread

cake

carrot

cheese

chicken

potatoes

rice

After reading

1 Look and order the story

2 Listen and say

Collins

Published by Collins
An imprint of HarperCollins*Publishers*
Westerhill Road
Bishopbriggs
Glasgow
G64 2QT

HarperCollins*Publishers*
1st Floor, Watermarque Building
Ringsend Road
Dublin 4
Ireland

William Collins' dream of knowledge for all began with the publication of his first book in 1819.

A self-educated mill worker, he not only enriched millions of lives, but also founded a flourishing publishing house. Today, staying true to this spirit, Collins books are packed with inspiration, innovation and practical expertise. They place you at the centre of a world of possibility and give you exactly what you need to explore it.

© HarperCollins*Publishers* Limited 2020

10 9 8 7 6 5 4 3 2

ISBN 978-0-00-839813-2

Collins® and COBUILD® are registered trademarks of HarperCollins*Publishers* Limited

www.collins.co.uk/elt

British Library Cataloguing in Publication Data

A catalogue record for this publication is available from the British Library.

Author: Julie Penn
Illustrator: Camilla Galindo (Beehive)
Series editor: Rebecca Adlard
Commissioning editor: Zoë Clarke
Publishing manager: Lisa Todd
Product managers: Jennifer Hall and Caroline Green
In-house editor: Alma Puts Keren
Project manager: Emily Hooton
Editor: Emma Wilkinson
Proofreaders: Natalie Murray and Michael Lamb
Cover designer: Kevin Robbins
Typesetter: 2Hoots Publishing Services Ltd
Audio produced by id audio, London
Reading guide author: Emma Wilkinson
Production controller: Rachel Weaver
Printed and bound by: GPS Group, Slovenia

MIX
Paper from
responsible sources
FSC™ C007454

This book is produced from independently certified FSC™ paper to ensure responsible forest management.

For more information visit: **www.harpercollins.co.uk/green**

Download the audio for this book and a reading guide for parents and teachers at www.collins.co.uk/839813